A TALE OF WITCHES

TAHIR SHAH

A TALE OF WITCHES

A Teaching Story

TAHIR SHAH

MMXXIV

Secretum Mundi Publishing Ltd
124 City Road
London
EC1V 2NX
United Kingdom

www.secretum-mundi.com
info@secretum-mundi.com

First published by Secretum Mundi Publishing Ltd, 2024
A version of this story originally appeared in *Scorpion Soup*, by Tahir Shah, 2013.

A TALE OF WITCHES

A CIP catalogue record for this title is available from the British Library.

ISBN 978-1-915876-51-5

VERSION 17042024

Visit the author's website:
Tahirshah.com

Who knows what a whale in the deep ocean dreams?

Ethiopian saying

Teaching Stories

When I was small, I was told stories from morning till night.

I was told stories about genies and witches and about great birds that could carry away elephants on their wings... and stories about distant kingdoms and magical lands ruled by warrior kings.

I was told stories of good and bad... stories of hope and others of despair.

I was even told stories about stories.

And all the while, I listened, amazed.

The more I listened, the more my mind worked... and the more I came to understand that these stories had a power about them, a secret lifeblood all of their own.

They were magical instruments, machineries that could alter states of mind and change the way we think.

But most importantly of all, stories can teach us, without us realizing that they are doing so at all.

Part of the default programming of man, stories are within us all.

Born into us, they make us who we are – they make us human.

Since earliest childhood, I have feasted on stories as a way of learning about the world, and learning about myself. They have been my dictionary and my encyclopaedia, my classroom, my guide, and my very best friend.

To descend down through the layers of stories is to be reborn, into a dominion of fantasy – one touched by real magic.

Pre-eminent within the great treasuries of tales, it is teaching stories like this one that have shown me the path to follow beyond the next horizon, and have made me the man I am.

Tahir Shah

Four wizened witches were clustered around a cauldron one night beneath the nocturnal firmament.

A little distance ahead was a chasm,
filled with the thunderclouds of a tempest.

The first of the hags was stirring the brew with a dead man's hand, the others tossing in ingredients for the spell.

‘Blood from a murdered child,’
whispered one.

'Pickled eye of an ostrich,'
cawed another.

‘Egg of an albino crocodile,’
hissed a third.

The severed hand stirred
seven times to the right…

… then seven to the left.

After a long span of silence, the first witch raised the hand in the air.

'It is ready,' she said solemnly.

Each of the witches jostled forwards.

The one who had been stirring
dipped the dead man’s hand into the brew.

And holding the cupped palm to her mouth,
she drank.

No sooner had the liquid touched her lips than the witch collapsed.

‘She is dead!’
cackled another of the crones.

'Serves her right!'
hooted the next.

The third fell silent and
jabbed a finger at the ground.

‘*L-l-l-l-look!*’
she stammered.

The witches peered down at their sister's body
and watched as, bathed in fire,
it began to change.

Layers of skin peeled back, then vanished.

Blood vessels showed themselves,
then muscles, tendons, and nerves.

As the tissue fell away,
a gleaming white skeleton was revealed.

The witch's sisters gasped
in both horror and delight.

‘She is being reborn,’
said one.

'Purity,'
said another.

‘And when she is pure she will have pure sight,’
winced a third.

Only when every trace of flesh had disappeared
did the skeleton begin to move.

With jerky movements, the torso sat upright,
a hand scratching the bones of the face…

… as the legs struggled to stand.

As it did so, the other sisters sat motionless, the cauldron's fire giving glow to their rapt expressions.

Slowly, the witch skeleton stood upright, even though it was lacking muscle and flesh.

Empty eye sockets scanned the
lengths of bone from elbow to wrist.

Then, glancing around,
it recognized the sisters.

'The potion has worked, my sisters,'
spoke the skeleton witch.
'I am ready to open the door.'

Turning, it ambled fitfully
to the sheering cliff face,
the bones of the arms outstretched.

'Mountain! O mountain,' the skeleton cried. 'I command you to reveal your sacred sanctuary!'

A minute passed.

Then another.

And, gradually, a magnificent circular doorway rose from the ground, its surface adorned with supernatural symbols.

The skeleton witch clapped its hands together three times and the door slid to the side.

Beyond it lay a passage,
lit by flaming torches.

Hurriedly, the skeleton stepped
forwards across the threshold.

As it did so, the door slid shut,
and the doorway itself vanished.

Inside the mountain, the skeleton witch
paced through the low tunnel.

Eventually it arrived at a staircase carved from granite, the steps covered in huge tarantulas.

Descending the stairs, the bones of its feet
crushing the spiders, the skeleton witch
took the steps one by one.

The stairway ended in a sheering wall
of carved lapis lazuli.

Once again, the witch skeleton clapped both hands together, and the stone barrier shattered, revealing a cavern illuminated by a great phosphorescent fire.

Running through the middle of the cavern was a boiling stream, its yellow waters sulphurous and rank.

Around its edge there were hundreds of large turquoise urns, each one overflowing with the ingredients for the dark arts.

Beside the fire stood a golden basin filled to the brim with squirming black scorpions.

Beside it was a pitcher.

Without haste, the skeleton witch filled
the pitcher from the stream and poured
the boiling liquid into the basin,
cooking the live scorpions.

When they had stewed well and good,
the skeleton witch touched the end of an
index digit into the liquid, allowing a single
drop of scorpion soup to tumble into its mouth.

Instantly, the skeleton grew arteries,
veins, muscles, and flesh.

But rather than being haggard as she had been,
the witch was restored to the radiance of her youth.

Her skin was pink and fresh,
her eyes bright green, her long
mane of hair vibrant and blonde.

Examining her delicate features in the broth's oily surface, the witch grinned approvingly.

‘At last,’ she said.

Gliding through the cavern,
she paused at a stone slab
at the east end of the chamber.

The sides were encrusted with smudged blood, as if someone, or something, had worked desperately to lift it.

Stooping down, the witch blew very softly,
and the stone crumbled into dust.

Beneath was a vast and imposing library
containing thousands and thousands
of grimy volumes.

Climbing down a ladder, the witch reached the parquet floor, and at once began hunting the book that she knew was there.

‘What are you searching for?’
said a voice.

The witch looked around.

'Who… who's there?'

'I am the library,' the voice replied. 'Tell me the book you wish for, and it shall be yours.'

‘A talking library?’
hissed the witch.

'All libraries speak,' replied the shelves,
'but not all who read can hear.'

'The spell to travel back in time,'
the witch uttered.
'Give it to me at once!'

A howling wind ripped through the chamber.

And, when it had come and gone,
an over-sized volume was sitting
squarely on the central table.

‘Page six hundred and nine,’
whispered the library’s voice.

The witch pulled back the cover…

Then, with care, she thumbed
her way through the book.

'Six hundred...' she said aloud,
'... and nine.'

Squinting to read the uneven print,
she scanned the page.

'This is no spell,'
she said tersely.

‘Of course it is,’ replied the library. ‘But to activate the spell you do not read it, but consume it.’

The witch frowned.
'I must eat it?'

The library grunted.
'The more of the spell you eat,
the further back in time you will travel.'

Without a second thought,
the witch ripped out the page.

She folded it again and again onto itself
as the library seemed to disappear
into the darkness of time.

Placing one half of the spell in her mouth,
she chewed and chewed.

And she swallowed.

A full minute of absolute tranquility passed.

Then, the witch dissolved into the air,
transported to a time and place
equating with the precise quantity
of the spell she had ingested.

The story does not conclude here.

Indeed, it continues for a thousand more pages.

But, in the land where this tale is told on perpetual winter nights, it is believed that the portion recounted must match the requirement of the audience.

And so, it is here that
A Tale of Witches draws to an end.

Finis

About the Author

Descended from a long line of storytellers, writers, and savants, Tahir Shah is one of the most prolific authors of his generation. He has published more than sixty books in numerous genres, including travel, fiction, and fantasy, as well as tales for children.

Raised in the tradition of Eastern 'teaching stories', Shah is passionate about stories and storytelling. He regards the ability to learn from folklore as being in us all, what he calls a 'default setting of humankind'. As well as having written scores of books, Shah has made documentaries for National Geographic TV and The History Channel. He is the founder and CEO of the charity, The Scheherazade Foundation.

Books By Tahir Shah

The Writer's Craft

The Reason to Write

Workbook: Comprehensive, Volume I & II

Workbook: Fantasy, Volume I & II

Workbook: Fiction, Volume I & II

Workbook: Historical Fiction, Volume I & II

Workbook: Teaching Stories, Volume I & II

Workbook: Travel, Volume I & II

Novels

Jinn Hunter: Book One – The Prism

Jinn Hunter: Book Two – The Jinnslayer

Jinn Hunter: Book Three – The Perplexity

Hannibal Fogg and the Supreme Secret of Man

Casablanca Blues

Eye Spy

Godman

Paris Syndrome

Timbuctoo

Midas

Zigzagzone

Nasrudin

Travels With Nasrudin

The Misadventures of the Mystifying Nasrudin

The Peregrinations of the Perplexing Nasrudin

The Voyages and Vicissitudes of Nasrudin

Nasrudin in the Land of Fools

Travel

Trail of Feathers

Travels With Myself

Beyond the Devil's Teeth

In Search of King Solomon's Mines

House of the Tiger King

In Arabian Nights

The Caliph's House

Sorcerer's Apprentice

Journey Through Namibia

Teaching Stories

The Arabian Nights Adventures

Scorpion Soup

Tales Told to a Melon

The Afghan Notebook

Daydreams of an Octopus & Other Stories

The Caravanserai Stories

Ghoul Brothers

Hourglass

Imaginist

Jinn's Treasure

Jinnlore

Mellified Man

Skeleton Island

Wellspring

When the Sun Forgot to Rise

Outrunning the Reaper

The Cap of Invisibility

On Backgammon Time

The Wondrous Seed

The Paradise Tree
Mouse House
The Hoopoe's Flight
The Old Wind
A Treasury of Tales
The Tale of Double Six
The Forgotten Game
King of the Jinns
The Destiny Ring
Changing the World
Cat, Mouse
Frogland
Mittle-Mittle
Capilongo
The Princess of Zilzilam
The Singing Serpents
The Tale of the Rusty Nail
The Unicorn's Tear
The Clockmaker Who Travelled Through Time
The Fish's Dream
The Man Whose Arms Grew Branches
The Most Foolish of Men
The Shop That Sold Truth
Qwerty
Renaissance
The Man With the Tiger's Head
The Kingdom of Blink
The Wisdom of Celestine
Dream Soup
The Skeleton Factory
An Unexpected Gift

The Problem Exchange
The Pharaoh Code
The Monkey Puzzle Club
Liquid Time
Cat Dog, Dog Cat
Princess Pickle's Laugh

Anthologies

The Anthologies: Africa
The Anthologies: Ceremony
The Anthologies: Childhood
The Anthologies: City
The Anthologies: Danger
The Anthologies: East
The Anthologies: Expedition
The Anthologies: Frontier
The Anthologies: Hinterland
The Anthologies: India
The Anthologies: Jinns
The Anthologies: Jungle
The Anthologies: Magic
The Anthologies: Morocco
The Anthologies: Nasrudin
The Anthologies: People
The Anthologies: Quest
The Anthologies: South
The Anthologies: Taboo
The Anthologies: Teaching Stories
The Clockmaker's Box
The Tahir Shah Fiction Reader
The Tahir Shah Travel Reader

Research

Cultural Research

The Middle East Bedside Book

Three Essays

Edited by

Congress With a Crocodile

A Son of a Son, Volume I

A Son of a Son, Volume II

Screenplays

Casablanca Blues: The Screenplay

Timbuctoo: The Screenplay

A REQUEST

If you enjoyed this book, please review it on your favourite online retailer or review website.

Reviews are an author's best friend.

To stay in touch with Tahir Shah, and to hear about his upcoming releases before anyone else, please sign up for his mailing list:

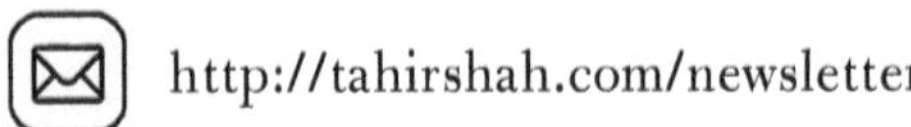

http://tahirshah.com/newsletter

And to follow him on social media, please go to any of the following links:

http://www.twitter.com/humanstew

@tahirshah999

http://www.facebook.com/TahirShahAuthor

http://www.youtube.com/user/tahirshah999

http://www.pinterest.com/tahirshah

https://www.goodreads.com/tahirshahauthor

http://www.tahirshah.com

www.ingramcontent.com/pod-product-compliance
Lightning Source LLC
Chambersburg PA
CBHW030522310726
48979CB00010B/1767/J

* 9 7 8 1 9 1 5 8 7 6 5 1 5 *